For Liz,
as we dance ever onward into our dotage.
— M. D.

For the dancer she once was.
— S.J. & L.F.

Viking

Published by Penguin Group
Penguin Young Readers Group, 345 Hudson Street, New York, New York 10014, U.S.A.
Penguin Group (Canada), 10 Alcorn Avenue, Toronto, Ontario, Canada M4V 3B2
(a division of Pearson Penguin Canada Inc.)
Penguin Books Ltd, 80 Strand, London WC2R 0RL, England
Penguin Ireland, 25 St Stephen's Green, Dublin 2, Ireland (a division of Penguin Books Ltd)
Penguin Group (Australia), 250 Camberwell Road, Camberwell, Victoria 3124, Australia
(a division of Pearson Australia Group Pty Ltd)
Penguin Books India Pvt Ltd, 11 Community Centre, Panchsheel Park, New Delhi – 110 017, India
Penguin Group (NZ), Cnr Airborne and Rosedale Roads, Albany, Auckland, New Zealand
(a division of Pearson New Zealand Ltd)
Penguin Books (South Africa) (Pty) Ltd, 24 Sturdee Avenue, Rosebank, Johannesburg 2196, South Africa

Penguin Books Ltd, Registered Offices: 80 Strand, London WC2R 0RL, England

First published in Great Britain in 2005 by Simon and Schuster UK Ltd
First published in the U.S.A. in 2005 by Viking, a division of Penguin Young Readers Group

3 5 7 9 10 8 6 4 2

Text copyright © Malachy Doyle, 2005
Illustrations copyright © Steve Johnson and Lou Fancher, 2005
All rights reserved

Library of Congress Cataloging-in-Publication Data is available.
ISBN 0-670-06020-8

Book design by Lou Fancher

Manufactured in China
Set in Nicolas-Jenson
The paintings are rendered in oil on paper.

The Dancing Tiger

by **Malachy Doyle**

paintings by **Steve Johnson** and **Lou Fancher**

Viking

There's a quiet, gentle tiger
In the woods below the hill,
And he dances on his tiptoes,
When the world is dreaming, still.

So you only ever hear him
In the silence of the night,
And you only ever see him
When the full moon's shining bright.

One summer night I saw him first,
Twirling, whirling round.
And then I heard him gasp in fright—
He knew that he'd been found.

*A*s he turned to me and whispered,
"Please don't mention that I'm here,"
The laughter in his lightning eyes
Swept away my fear.

"*I*f you will keep me secret,
And never tell a soul,
Then you may come and dance with me
On nights the moon is whole."

So once a month, from then till now,
I've tiptoed to the wood.
We've swirled and swayed among the trees,
As Tiger said we could.

We've skipped in spring through bluebells,

*I*n summer circled slow,

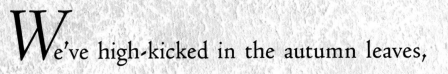

We've high-kicked in the autumn leaves,

*A*nd waltzed in winter snow.

But now that I am old and gray,
My dancing nights are done.
I've chosen you, great-grandchild,
To take my place, so come . . .

Let me give you Tiger's hand—
The moon is rising high.
I'll sit and watch you dancing both,
Beneath the starbright sky.